D0794665

This book is for my amazing daughter Isla, who asked me to write her a story about Witches. She also helped me produce it!

The Witches' Tea Party

Written by Stuart McDonald

Published by Amazon KDP 2019

ISBN: 9781724440761

Heggerty Witch was making a list,
Of treats that witches can't resist.

Her friends were invited around for a meal,
They were all very fussy, so it had to appeal!

She wrote down the things she knew she would need.
She had five hungry witches expecting a feed!

"A starter," she thought. "Something simple and light."
Then she had it. "Oh yes that'll do just right!"

"Frog Surprise!" she said with such glee.
"That'll make a lovely start to our tea!"

Six frogs were added to the shopping list.
And housefly jam, for that extra twist.

"Now the main course. " she said scratching her chin.
"Something quite filling": they're all very thin.

She looked in the cupboards to get some ideas.
"I've got it!" she shrieked.
"I'll make Bat Ear Tortillas!"

So onto the list went six long eared bats.
Two ears each, for her friends in tall hats.

The starter was chosen, and so was the main.
But what for dessert? She racked her brain.

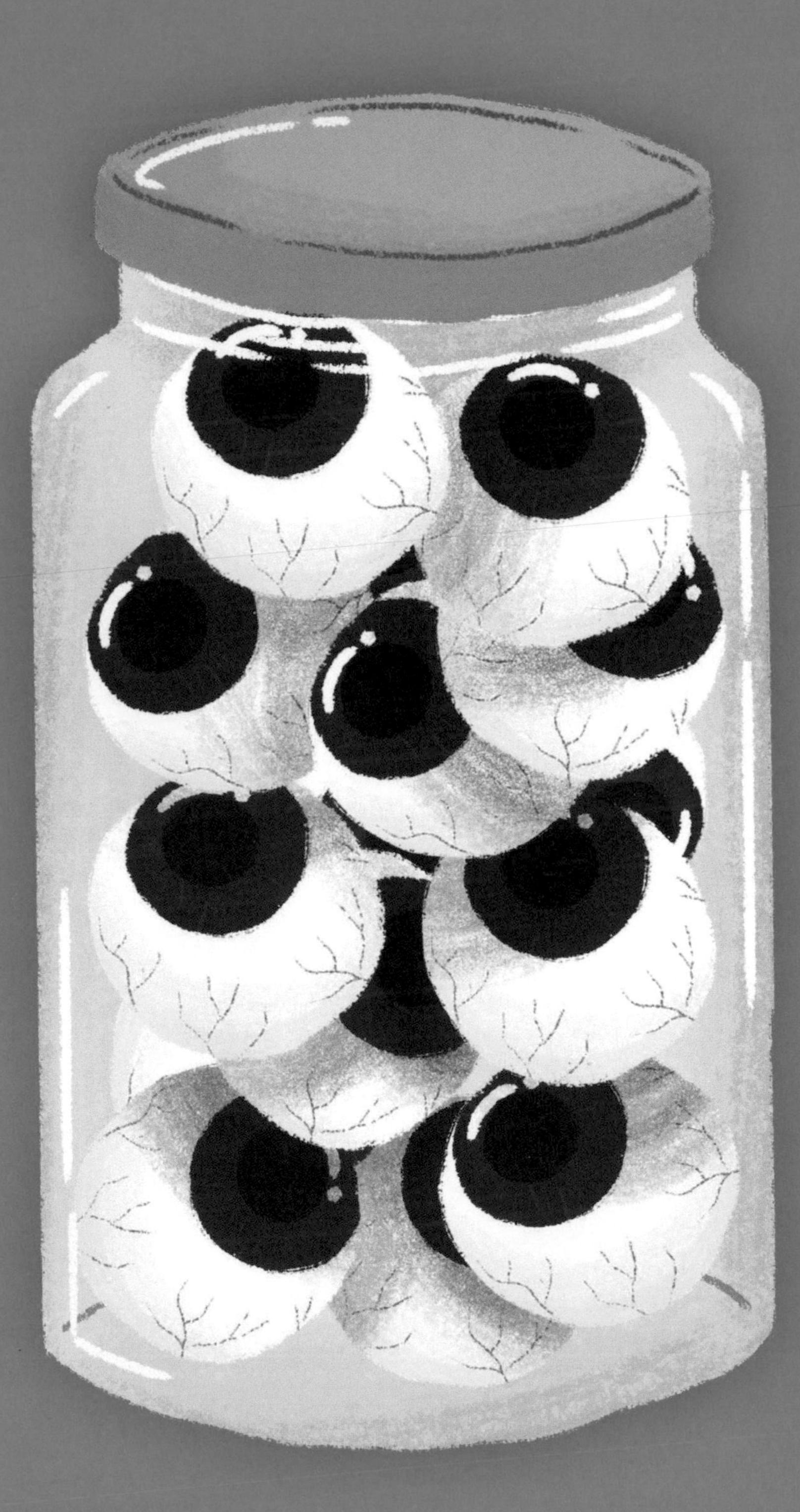

It had to be special. Something outstanding!
Her warty-nosed friends were very demanding!

It had to be something they'd never forget.
An amazing creation from her kitchenette!

A cake? A pudding? A trifle with cream?
"That's it!" Heggerty squealed.
"Special Eye Scream!"

So last on the list went a jar full of eyes!
That was sure to give them a lovely surprise!

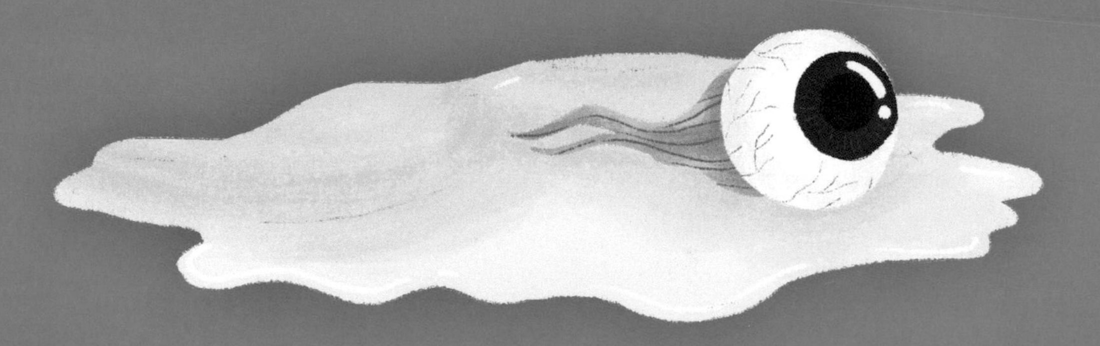

She grabbed her cauldron and jumped on her broom.
And flew to the Spookermarket by the light of the moon.

In no time at all she returned with her goods.
It wasn't that far away; just through the woods.

She set about prepping and chopping and stirring.
With Fidget the cat at her feet, purring.

Her hard-to-please friends would arrive in an hour.
The place was a mess, she was covered in flour!

A quick spell was needed to sort the place out.
So Heggerty thought and then blurted one out.

"Soap and polish, duster and broom,
Work hard together to tidy this room!"

"Scrub it and brush it and make this room gleam,
Do not stop 'til it's fit for a queen!"

Her spell was answered and soon the room shone!
All of the mess and the flour were gone.

Just in time too as the clock just struck four.
Then came a very loud knock at the door.

Agatha was the first witch to arrive.
As she'd broken her broom she'd decided to drive.

"Am I early?" she asked as she entered the room.
"Right on time," said Heggerty.
"But where is your broom?"

"I broke it again," said poor Agatha sighing.
"I think a new one I'll soon be buying!"

Before they could settle another knock came.
This time it was Mordrid and she'd brought a game.

Then Ingrid and Willow and Sybil came in.
"Great!" squealed Heggerty "Let the party begin!"

They all took their places and sat down to eat.
While Fidget the cat fussed around at their feet.

The Frog Surprise was an absolute hit!
They really enjoyed it; they had to admit.

The Bat Ear Tortillas were popular as well.
The taste was amazing, and so was the smell!

The witches were all being very polite.
Heggerty was having such a good night!

She brought out dessert; her Special Eye Scream.
Each bowl had three scoops with some eyes inbetween!

They wolfed it all down, 'til no eyeballs remained.
No-one was grumbling. No-one complained.

Then without witchcraft or spells of any kind.
Her friends did the dishes until they all shined.

Heggerty smiled as they showed gratitude!
Her hard-to-please friends were no longer rude.

"You must come again!" she gleefully cried!
"And we'll cook for you!" the witches replied.

Special thanks must go to my dear friend Joc,
for her 'marvy' magic spell checking! xxx